STERLING CHILDREN'S BOOKS
New York

An Imprint of Sterling Publishing
387 Park Avenue South
New York, NY 10016

© 2013 by Sterling Publishing Co., Inc.
Design by Jennifer Browning

ISBN 978-1-4027-8341-8

Library of Congress Cataloging-in-Publication Data Available

Distributed in Canada by Sterling Publishing
c/o Canadian Manda Group, 165 Dufferin Street
Toronto, Ontario, Canada M6K 3H6
Distributed in the United Kingdom by GMC Distribution Services
Castle Place, 166 High Street, Lewes, East Sussex, England BN7 1XU
Distributed in Australia by Capricorn Link (Australia) Pty. Ltd.
P.O. Box 704, Windsor, NSW 2756, Australia

For information about custom editions, special sales, and premium and corporate
purchases, please contact Sterling Special Sales at 800-805-5489
or specialsales@sterlingpublishing.com.

Printed in China
Lot #:
2 4 6 8 10 9 7 5 3 1
07/13

www.sterlingpublishing.com/kids

SILVER PENNY STORIES

Sleeping Beauty

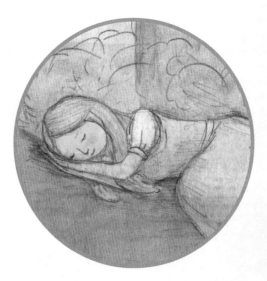

Told by Deanna McFadden
Illustrated by Stephanie Graegin

Once upon a time, a king and queen gave birth to a baby girl. They named her Briar Rose. The king and queen ordered a great feast so the entire kingdom could celebrate.

The king wanted to invite the
thirteen wise women of the kingdom,
but he had only twelve golden plates.
So the thirteenth wise woman
was not invited.

On the day of the feast, each wise woman stepped forward to give a wonderful gift to the princess. The first gave the princess goodness. The second gave beauty. The other wise women stepped forward to offer their gifts to the child.

Suddenly, a cloud of smoke appeared. When it cleared, there stood the thirteenth wise woman.

Furious that she wasn't invited to the feast, she cursed the princess.

"When this child turns fifteen, she will prick her finger on a spindle and fall down dead!" the thirteenth wise woman shouted.

Then she disappeared in a cloud of smoke.

The twelfth wise woman had not yet given her gift. Even though she could not undo the curse, she said, "The princess will not die, but will fall into a deep sleep that will last one hundred years."

The king and queen were
heartbroken and wanted to prevent
the disaster. The king ordered all
the spindles in the kingdom to be
destroyed so nothing would happen
to the princess.

Princess Briar Rose grew into a beautiful young woman. On her fifteenth birthday, her parents were called away from the kingdom. The king and queen had not forgotten the thirteenth wise woman's curse, so they said to Briar Rose, "Do not wander around the castle today without us."

But the princess had never been alone before. She decided to explore all the hidden corners of the castle, and she climbed to the top of one of its towers. There she found a heavy door with a rusty key in the lock. She turned the key and entered a tiny room where an old woman was sitting at a spinning wheel.

The princess asked, "What are
you doing?"

The old woman replied,
"I'm spinning wool, my dear."

Curious, the princess reached her
hand forward and pricked her finger
on the spindle.

Immediately, the princess fell into a deep sleep. A cloud of smoke rose up, and the old woman turned back into the thirteenth wise woman. The evil woman saw that the princess was not dead, but just sleeping.

Furious that her curse had been changed, the thirteenth wise woman raised her hands and spread the sleeping spell over the entire castle. Then she placed a thick hedge of thorns around the castle so no one could enter.

The king and queen had just returned, and they fell asleep instantly. Their royal horses fell asleep in their stables. The dogs fell asleep in the courtyard. Even the wind stopped blowing.

Stories spread about Sleeping Beauty, the beautiful princess cursed to sleep for one hundred years.

Every prince in the land wanted to save Sleeping Beauty. They came from far away to fight their way through the hedge around the castle. But none ever made it through.

One day, a brave young prince was traveling through the kingdom. He met an old man who told him the story of Sleeping Beauty.

"I'm going to find the castle and free the princess," he said.

When the prince arrived, he found beautiful flowers instead of the hedge of thorns. One hundred years had passed, and the curse was fading.

Inside the courtyard, the prince found some sleeping dogs and sleeping horses. He climbed the tower and found the little room where Sleeping Beauty lay.

Sleeping Beauty was so beautiful, the prince couldn't take his eyes off her. He bent down to kiss her. At that moment, she woke up and smiled at him. The prince took her hand and led Sleeping Beauty out of the little room.

The king and queen woke up. Their royal horses woke up in their stables. The animals in the courtyard woke up. The breeze began to blow again.

The king and queen were overjoyed to see their daughter with the handsome young prince who had broken the spell.

They declared a celebration throughout the land for the marriage of Sleeping Beauty and the prince. The evil thirteenth wise woman was never heard from again.

And the prince and Sleeping Beauty lived happily ever after.